STORIES FROM

SPAIN

Folklore of the World

Each of the Folklore of the World Books contains carefully selected myths and folktales most representative of a single country. These books will help children to understand people in other lands and will help them to develop an appreciation for their customs and culture. Peace for the world can come only through the spreading of this understanding and appreciation.

The Folklore Books are the third step in the Dolch program, *Steps to a Lifetime Reading Habit.* The series on these graded steps, starting with the most elementary, are: the First Reading Books, the Basic Vocabulary Books, the Folklore of the World Books, and the Pleasure Reading Books.

Folklore Books are prepared under the direction of Edward W. Dolch, formerly Professor of Education, University of Illinois. In all the series, emphasis is placed on good storytelling and literary quality, as well as on simplicity of vocabulary.

Books in this series are (to date):

- Stories from Alaska
- Stories from Canada
- Stories from France
- Stories from Hawaii
- Stories from India
- Stories from Italy
- Stories from Japan
- Stories from Mexico
- Stories from Old China
- Stories from Old Egypt
- Stories from Old Russia
- Stories from Spain

STORIES FROM SPAIN

Folklore of the World

by EDWARD W. DOLCH
and MARGUERITE P. DOLCH
illustrated by
DON BOLOGNESE

GARRARD PUBLISHING COMPANY
CHAMPAIGN, ILLINOIS

Library of Congress No.: 62-7207

MANUFACTURED IN THE UNITED STATES OF AMERICA

Foreword

Spain includes many different types of country, from the warm lands of the south to the mountainous sections of the north. At one time, the different parts of the country were different kingdoms. Each of these kingdoms had its own folklore, and these are all represented in this collection. The local color of the different parts of the country is seen in the things mentioned in the stories, such as oranges, silver mines, mountain caves, and so on.

A special characteristic of the country is the contribution of the culture of the Moors, who at one time ruled part of southern Spain. There is a great wealth of Moorish tales, only a few of which could be included for lack of space. More of these tales can be found in such books as Washington Irving's Tales of the Alhambra.

Spain has also many hero-tales from the Middle Ages. We have been able to give only one, a part of the picturesque career of the great hero, the Cid.

We trust these stories will show something of the interest and charm of Spanish folklore, and that they may lead the reader to seek out some of the many books of these stories.

E. W. DOLCH

Santa Barbara, Calif.

Contents

POTIONS
AND

The Basket of Pears

Once upon a time there was a King of Spain who had only one daughter. She was a beautiful girl. But she was always sick.

The King called all the wise men and all the doctors in his country to come and see the Princess. The doctors could do nothing. But the wise men said,

"The Princess must eat the most beautiful pears in Spain. Then the Princess will get well."

The King sent word all over Spain. He told the people,

"Take to the King the most beautiful pears that you have. If your pears make the Princess well, the King will give you anything that you wish."

Many people took pears to the King. The Princess ate the pears, but she did not get well.

In a small village lived a farmer with three sons. The father had a pear tree that he thought was the finest pear tree in Spain.

One day, the father said to the oldest son,

"My son, I am sure that the finest pears in Spain grow on my pear tree. Take a basket of pears to the King. If the pears make the Princess well, you can ask of the King anything that you wish."

The oldest son picked a basket of pears and covered it with a white cloth. He started for the castle of the King of Spain. On the road to the palace, he met a woman and a little girl. They looked tired and hungry.

"Where are you going?" asked the old woman.

"Why should I tell you?" said the oldest son.

"What is in your basket?" asked the old woman.

The oldest son did not want to

tell the woman that he was carrying a basket of pears. She might want some of his pears to eat, for she and the little girl looked both tired and hungry. So he said,

"These are horns in my basket."

The woman said, "Let them be horns."

When the oldest son got to the palace, he was taken before the King.

"I bring the Princess a basket of my father's pears," said the oldest son. He took the white cloth from off his basket.

The oldest son had a basket of horns.

The King was very angry. He had the oldest son put in a dungeon under the castle.

When the oldest son did not come back, the father said to the second son,

"Something has happened to your brother. I want you to take a basket of pears to the King. I want you to find out what has happened to your brother."

The second son picked a basket of pears and covered them with a white cloth. He started for the castle of the King of Spain. On the road to the palace, he met the woman and the little girl.

"Where are you going?" asked the woman.

"Why should I tell you?" said the second son.

"What is in your basket?" asked the old woman.

The second son did not want to tell the old woman that he was carrying a basket of pears. So he said,

"There are stones in my basket."

The old woman said, "Let them be stones."

When the second son got to the castle, he was taken before the King.

"I bring the Princess a basket of my father's pears," said the second son. And he took the white cloth from off his basket.

The second son had a basket of stones.

The King was very angry. He had the second son put in a dungeon under the castle.

The Princess Is Well

The father whose sons had taken pears to the Princess waited and waited. But his sons did not come home. At last the youngest son, whose name was Pedro, began to pick a basket of pears.

"What are you doing?" asked the father.

"I am picking a basket of pears to take to the Princess. I am sure that these yellow pears will make her well."

"You must not go," said the father. "Your brothers did not

come back. Now I have only you to help me."

"I will find my brothers," said Pedro. "They will come back and help you on the farm."

Pedro picked the most beautiful pears on the pear tree. He put the pears in a basket and covered them with a white cloth. Then he started for the castle of the King of Spain. On the road he met the woman and the little girl. They looked tired and hungry.

"Where are you going?" asked the old woman.

"I am going to the castle of the King of Spain," said Pedro.

"What is in your basket?" asked the old woman.

"I have yellow pears for the Princess. I am sure that my pears will make her well," said Pedro.

Pedro thought to himself, "The old woman and the little girl look tired and hungry." So Pedro gave the little girl a yellow pear.

"Thank you," said the old woman. "Your yellow pears will make the Princess well again." Then she said to Pedro, "Now ask what you wish and I will give it to you."

"I love the animals that live in the woods," said Pedro. "I wish

I had a whistle which would call any animal to me."

"Here it is," said the old woman. She opened her hand and there lay a silver whistle. Pedro thanked the old woman and put the whistle in his pocket. And off he went to the castle of the King of Spain.

When Pedro got to the castle, he was taken before the King.

"I bring the Princess a basket of my father's pears," said Pedro. And he took the white cloth from off his basket.

The King and the Princess had never seen such beautiful yellow pears.

"You have brought the Princess the most beautiful pears in Spain," said the King.

The Princess ate one pear. She ate two pears. She ate three pears.

"I do not feel sick any more," said the Princess. "I have eaten the most beautiful pears in Spain and I am well."

"Ask for anything that you want," said the King.

"I want my two brothers," said Pedro. "They must go home and help my father on the farm."

"I will send your brothers home at once," said the King.

The King looked at his beautiful

daughter. She was so well and happy. He said to Pedro, "I will give you another wish."

"If I have another wish," said Pedro, "I want to marry the princess."

"She cannot marry the son of a farmer," said the King.

"But I am not just the son of a farmer," said Pedro. "I will show you that I can do something that no one else in the world can do."

Pedro went into the woods around the King's castle. He took the silver whistle out of his pocket and blew upon it. He called a hare to him. He took the hare to the King and said,

"Put a mark upon this hare, so that you know that he is yours. Then let him run into the woods. In a year, I will come back and call him to you."

"You cannot call a hare to come to you," said the King. "That is magic. But in a year if you can call this hare to you, I will let you marry the Princess."

The Bag of Truth

Pedro lived in the woods for a year. He made friends with all the animals, for he called them to him with his silver whistle.

At the end of the year, Pedro went back to the castle of the King of Spain. As he was walking through the woods near the castle, he called the hare with the King's mark upon it. He took the hare in his arms and walked to the castle.

The King of Spain was looking

out of the window of the castle. He saw Pedro with the hare in his arms. Then the King remembered what he had said to Pedro a year ago.

"You cannot call a hare to you. That is magic. But in a year if you can call this hare to you, I will let you marry the Princess."

The King of Spain did not want the Princess to marry the son of a farmer. He must get that hare away from Pedro.

The King sent for his servant. "Take this bag of gold. Go buy that hare if it has my mark upon it."

The servant went out of the castle and met Pedro carrying the hare with the King's mark upon it. The servant gave Pedro the bag of gold and Pedro gave him the hare. But before the servant could get back into the castle Pedro blew his silver whistle. The hare came back to Pedro.

The King was watching from his window. When he saw that Pedro again had the hare in his arms, he did not know what to do.

"I will send the Princess to Pedro. He will give the hare to the Princess," said the King.

The Princess went to meet Pedro.

"Dear Princess," said Pedro, "I love you very much, but I cannot give you the hare with the King's mark upon it. Your father must come to meet me for he made me a promise a year ago."

Pedro would not give the hare to the Princess.

So the King went to meet Pedro. "I will give you ten bags of gold for that hare," said the King.

"You can have the hare for nothing, if you will kiss him," said Pedro.

The King was very angry. But he had to have the hare.

"Is anyone looking?" said the King.

"No," said Pedro. "No one is looking."

The King went behind a tree and kissed the hare.

Then the King with the hare in his arms went into the castle. Pedro followed the King inside. They went into a large room where the men and women of the court were sitting.

Pedro said to everyone, "Now the King of Spain can keep his promise to me. I wish to marry the Princess."

The people of the court were

very much surprised. They had never heard of the son of a farmer marrying a Princess. The King did not know what to do. He knew that a King should always keep his promise. But he did not want the Princess to marry the son of a farmer. Then the King had a happy thought. "There is one thing you must do before you marry the Princess," said the King. "You must take a big bag and fill it with Truth."

"Get me a big bag," said Pedro. "I shall be glad to fill it with Truth."

The servants got the biggest

bag they could find and gave it to Pedro.

"I can fill this bag with Truth right here in the castle," said Pedro.

He opened the bag and said to the King,

"Is it true that I brought a basket of the most beautiful pears in Spain to the Princess?"

"Yes," said the King. "That is the truth."

"Truth," said Pedro, "go into the bag."

"Is it true that those pears made the Princess well?" asked Pedro.

"Yes," said the King, "That is the truth."

"Truth," said Pedro, "go into the bag."

"Is it true that I gave the King a hare as a sign of the promise that he gave me?" said Pedro.

"Yes," said the King, "that is the truth."

"Truth," said Pedro, "go into the bag."

"Is it true that the King put his mark upon the hare and then let it run away to the woods? Is it true that I brought this hare back to the King?" asked Pedro.

"Yes," said the King, "that is true."

"Truth," said Pedro, "go into the bag."

Pedro looked hard at the King.

"Is it true," asked Pedro, "that the King wanted to get out of his promise and that he kissed –"

"Stop, stop," cried the King. "The bag is full of truth. You may marry the Princess."

So Pedro and the Princess were married, and they lived happily ever after.

Who Does the Work?

Long, long ago, there was an old man and his wife who lived on a farm. The wife worked in her house from morning until night. But the old man never seemed to do any work on his farm.

The old man's farm was the best farm in the countryside. But the other farmers never saw the old man working on his farm.

When the wife went to the river to wash the clothes, the neighbors would ask her,

"Who does the work on your farm?"

But the wife never saw her husband working. She did not know who did the work on the farm. And her husband would not tell her the secret.

One Sunday the farmer and his wife were going to church. The farmer walked ahead and the wife walked behind. The wife saw her husband hide something in the bushes beside the road. The wife said to herself,

"I am sure that my husband's secret is in the bushes."

The farmer walked on down the road. His wife called to him,

"I must go back to the house, for I left the pot on the fire."

So the farmer went on down the road, and the wife turned back. She looked under the bushes where her husband had been. And there she found a little gold box. She opened it. And out of the gold box came ten big flies.

The flies buzzed and buzzed about the woman's head. She heard them crying,

"What are we to do? What are we to do?"

The woman was very much afraid and she cried,

"Go back into the box! Go back into the box!"

She was very much surprised, for the ten big flies went into the box at once. She put the gold box back under the bush. Then she went on to church.

When the farmer and his wife were coming home from church, the wife said,

"I found your gold box under the bushes beside the road."

"Then I will have to tell you the secret of my fairy flies," said the farmer. "My fairy flies do all my work. There is only one thing that I must do. I must always have work for them to do."

"The fairy flies can do my work too," said the wife.

From that day, the neighbors never saw the farmer or his wife do any work. The wife never came to the river to wash clothes. The farmer never went to his hay field.

The wife of the farmer was not happy. She had nothing to do. All day long the fairy flies buzzed about her head, calling, "What are we to do?"

The fairy flies did all the work so quickly that the poor woman could not think of more things for them to do. She went to the farmer and said,

"I cannot stand these fairy flies. I want to do my own work."

The farmer was tired out too from trying to find work for the fairy flies to do.

"We must pay the fairy flies," said the farmer.

"I will give them my ten fine geese," said the woman.

The farmer called the ten fairy flies to him.

"We cannot find more work for you to do," he said. "But we give you our ten fine geese."

Just then the ten fine geese flew up into the air. And the ten fairy flies flew after them.

The farmer worked on his farm. He cut his hay and the neighbors came and talked to him. But he never told anyone about the ten fairy flies.

The farmer's wife worked from morning until night. Her house was always clean. When she went to the river to wash the clothes, she talked with her neighbors.

But she never told anyone about the ten fairy flies.

Father Crow and Mother Crow

On a cliff by the King's palace, there grew a tall tree. In this tree there was a crow's nest.

Father Crow and Mother Crow had a very fine nest. Year after year they had a family of little ones. The two crows would have been very happy but for one thing.

Half way up the cliff lived a snake. When this snake got hungry, he crawled up the cliff. He waited until Father Crow and Mother

Crow were away. Then he crawled up and ate the baby crows.

Father Crow got very angry. "I am tired of feeding that snake with our baby crows," he said. "We are never going to have a family in this nest again." And he began to pull the nest to pieces.

"Do not pull our nest to pieces," said Mother Crow. "I must think of some way to kill that snake."

"How can a crow kill a snake?" said Father Crow.

"I will sit on my nest until the Good God tells me how I can kill that snake," said Mother Crow.

Father Crow was very angry.

"Sit on the nest if you like," said Father Crow. "But I am going to fly to the King's garden and find something to eat."

Mother Crow got very tired of sitting on the nest. When Father Crow came back, she said,

"The King's garden is very beautiful."

"Yes," said Father Crow. "The King's garden is very beautiful. But the most beautiful thing in the King's garden is the Princess. And the most beautiful thing about the Princess is the crown upon her head."

"The Good God has told me how to kill the snake," said Mother Crow. "Come with me and do just what I tell you to do."

Mother Crow flew to the King's garden. Father Crow followed her.

The Princess was playing with a ball in the garden. The ladies-in-waiting were talking together. The two crows were flying around the Princess.

The Princess stopped playing with her ball. She looked up and watched the crows. And suddenly her crown fell onto the grass.

"Father Crow," called Mother

Crow. "Help me carry the crown back to our nest."

The Princess cried. The Ladies-in-waiting called the soldiers. They watched the two crows carry the crown to the nest in the tall tree.

"Do not cry, Little Princess," said the soldiers. "We will get your crown for you."

The two crows sat in their nest on top of the crown. The Father Crow was very angry.

"What good is a crown to us? We cannot eat it."

"Wait and see what happens," said the Mother Crow. "The Good God told me to take the crown."

"The King's soldiers will come and get the crown," said Father Crow. "They will pull our nest out of the tree."

"Wait and see," said Mother Crow.

The two crows could hear the soldiers at the bottom of the cliff. Slowly the soldiers climbed the cliff.

When the first soldier was half way up the cliff, he called,

"I have found a big snake asleep. What shall we do?"

"Kill it," said the second soldier. "It might crawl into the King's garden and hurt the Princess."

The first soldier took his sword and killed the snake.

Then the two crows took the crown and put it at the foot of the tree. When the soldiers got to the top of the cliff, they found the crown. They took it back to the Princess.

The two crows sat on their nest.

"Now we can have another family," said Mother Crow. "There will be no snake to kill the little ones."

"The Good God will look after us," said Father Crow. And he made the nest good and strong for another family.

The Magic Stick

Once upon a time an old man named Calamin lived beside a river. Every day he went down to the river. Sometimes he found bits of gold in the sands of the river.

Calamin was sure that the bits of gold came from some place up in the mountains. He wanted more than anything else to find where the gold came from.

One day Calamin sent some men to dig on the side of the mountain where he thought the gold might be. The men dug all day and made a big hole. The sun went down, and the men went home. In the morning, the hole was filled with dirt.

"There is magic on this mountainside," said the men. "We will not dig on the mountain again."

After that, no one would go up on the mountainside.

Near the old miser, Calamin, lived a young doctor. He was a good man and a happy man. Everyone in the countryside knew Jose Mari, the young doctor.

One day Jose Mari was going to the village. He was walking along the road singing to himself.

He called to Calamin and wished him good morning. But Calamin did not have a good word for anyone.

As Jose Mari went along the road, he met two young men.

"Are you going to the village?" asked one of the young men.

"Yes," said the doctor.

"May we walk with you?" said the other young man.

"Yes," said the doctor. "I see that you are strangers to this countryside." For the doctor knew all the people of the countryside.

"We live nearby," said one of the young men.

The three young men walked to the village together. When they got to the village, the two strangers bought three fine cows. They gave one of them to Jose Mari.

The sun had gone down when the three young men started home. Each man was leading a cow. And they sang as they walked along.

It was dark as they came to a big rock beside the road.

"Friend Jose, we must leave you now," said one of the strangers.

"We are the Princes of the Otherside," said the other stranger. "We must go to our kingdom. But we would like you to come to see us. Take this magic stick. If ever you want to come to the Kingdom of the Otherside, hit this rock seven times with the magic stick. The rock will open."

Jose Mari could not believe his eyes. The big rock opened. The two young men, leading the two cows, walked through the rock and disappeared into the mountain. Then the rock closed.

Jose Mari looked again. He saw a big rock beside the road. He was holding a little stick in his hand, and he was leading a fine cow.

The Sick Princess

One day, Jose Mari, the young doctor, knew that he must go to the Kingdom of the Otherside. He was sure that his friends needed him.

Jose Mari went to the big rock beside the road. He hit the rock seven times with his magic stick. The rock opened. The young doctor stepped quickly inside. Then he fell down, down, down into the Kingdom of the Otherside.

Jose Mari landed on a bed of flowers. It was as bright as day!

He looked around him at a beautiful garden. He heard someone laughing. His two friends were looking down at him as he lay in the flower bed.

"My name is Beltram," said one of the young men. "Welcome to the Kingdom of the Otherside. This is my brother, Camilo."

"The little birds told me that you were coming," said Camilo. "We are very glad to see you, for our sister is sick."

"You are a doctor and we are sure that you can make her well," said Beltram.

Jose Mari got to his feet. He shook hands with the two brothers.

"Take me to your sister. I will be glad to see what I can do for her," he said.

"First, you must put on these boots," said Camilo.

He gave Jose Mari some golden boots. When he put on the boots, he started to go up in the air.

The two brothers laughed and took Jose Mari's hands.

"You will have to get used to the way to walk in the Kingdom of the Otherside," said Beltram.

Jose Mari felt as light as a

feather. He moved his legs and put one foot before the other. But he felt as if he were flying. Beltram and Camilo kept hold of his hands. In a short time they came to a beautiful palace. It looked as if it were made of gold.

The two brothers and the doctor went into the palace. They went to the room of the Princess Aurea, where she lay sick in bed.

"My dear sister," said Beltram, "we have brought our friend, the doctor, to see you. He will help you to get well."

The Princess smiled and held out her hand.

"Welcome to our Kingdom of the Otherside," she said.

Jose Mari looked at the Princess very carefully. Then he said,

"I will give you some pills. You are to take two pills every time a bird flies past your window. You will soon be well again. And tell me what you like to do most of all?"

"I like to swim and I like to dance. I like to lie on the grass and look up at the birds in the trees. And most of all I like to read a good book."

"We will let you lie on the grass and read a good book," said the doctor. "And when you are stronger, we will let you swim and dance. You will soon be well."

"Thank you for coming to see me," said Princess Aurea. "I feel better already."

Beltram and Camilo took Jose Mari to a big rock that stood in the palace garden. They gave him a bag of gold dust for a present.

"Thank you for coming to see our sister," said Beltram. "I am sure that she is going to get well."

"You must not tell anyone of your visit to the Kingdom of the Otherside," said Camilo. "By the laws of our country, anyone who tells is put to death. Remember not to tell anyone where you got the gold dust."

The big rock in the palace garden opened, and Jose Mari went through it. He went up and up and up. Suddenly, he found himself on the road near his house. And he was carrying a bag of gold dust.

The Treasure

Jose Mari, the young doctor, was coming home after his visit to the Kingdom of the Otherside. He was walking up the road, carrying a bag of gold dust. On the road, he met the old miser.

"How are you feeling, Neighbor Calamin?" said the doctor.

"I am feeling very sick," said Calamin. "I cannot sleep. All night long, I think about the gold somewhere on the mountainside."

"Walk with me to my house," said the doctor, "and I will give you some pills to make you feel better."

Calamin kept looking at the bag that the doctor carried. He could see bits of gold on the bag.

"This morning I saw you go up the road to the big rock," said Calamin, "and when I followed you, I could not see you, for you had disappeared."

Jose Mari did not know what to say.

"I think that you are a doctor of magic," said Calamin. "I think that you know the secret of the gold in the mountainside."

"Old man," said the doctor, "I

think that you are sick. Come into my house and I will give you some pills."

Jose Mari and Calamin went into the house. Jose Mari put the bag on the table.

"Give me that bag of gold," said Calamin, "or I will tell the people of the village that you are a doctor of magic, and they will burn you to death."

Jose Mari was very much afraid. He knew that if old Calamin told the people that he was a doctor of magic, they would burn him to death. And so he gave Calamin the bag.

The old miser opened the bag. And he let out a cry.

"You have fooled me by your magic," he cried. "There is nothing in the bag but ashes."

Jose Mari was very angry.

"Yes, the bag is full of ashes," he cried. "I get the ashes in the woods to make my pills."

Jose Mari was so angry that he took a handful of the ashes and threw it at Calamin. But as soon as Jose Mari touched the ashes, they were turned into gold dust.

"Now I know that you are a doctor of magic," cried Calamin. "You can turn ashes into gold.

The people of the village will burn you to death."

Jose Mari knew that he would have to tell Calamin about the Kingdom of the Otherside or he would be burned to death. So he told the story to Calamin.

"You must take me to the Kingdom of the Otherside," said Calamin. "I must see the gold."

At last Jose Mari said that he would take the old miser to the Kingdom of the Otherside. He hoped that the Princess Aurea would forgive him for telling the secret of the Otherside.

"I must first go to my home,"

said Calamin. "I want to write a letter. If I do not come back, I want the people to know that you are a doctor of magic."

After Calamin had written the letter, he put a long dagger in his belt and said,

"I am ready to go to the Kingdom of the Otherside. And if you do not take me to the gold, I will kill you with this dagger."

Jose Mari and Calamin went to the big rock beside the road. Jose Mari hit the rock seven times with the magic stick, and it opened. Jose Mari and Calamin walked through. Down, down,

down they fell to the Kingdom of the Otherside.

Jose Mari did not fall into a flower bed this time. He fell into the middle of the courtyard of the palace. Calamin had fallen beside him. But the long dagger that he had put into his belt had gone right through him. He was dead.

Jose Mari looked up. He saw a tall man dressed in black looking at him.

"You did not keep the secret of the Otherside," said the man. "Our law says that you must die. But you made our Princess well again. And she says that you may go back to the Outside. Never again will you be able to come to the Kingdom of the Otherside."

All at once, Jose Mari found himself on the road to his house. He felt sick. He could hardly walk. So he sat down on a stone beside the road.

"Oh, if I could only have stayed in the Kingdom of the Otherside," he said to himself. "Now the people of the village will find the letter that Calamin wrote calling me a doctor of magic. I will be burned to death."

As Jose Mari sat beside the road, he saw that a house was on fire. It was Calamin's house and it burned to the ground.

Then the doctor knew that he was saved. No one would find the letter. No one would know about the bag of gold dust. And no one would call him a doctor of magic.

Jose Mari ran home. There he found the cow that the Princes of the Kingdom of the Otherside had given him. How glad he was that she had not disappeared.

And the cow gave him fine milk for his supper.

The Three Oranges

Once upon a time there was a little Prince who loved to tease people. One morning he was sitting by the fountain throwing stones into the water. An old woman called La Mora came to the fountain to get water.

"Do not throw any stones into the fountain or you will break my pitcher," said La Mora.

The Prince only laughed and threw more stones into the fountain. And one of the stones broke the old woman's pitcher.

La Mora was very angry.

"Little Prince, when you grow up, you shall never rest until you find the Three Oranges."

The Prince laughed at La Mora and for years he forgot about the Three Oranges.

La Mora was a witch. And what a witch says often happens. And so when the Prince became a young man, he could find no rest.

One day the Prince went to the King and said,

"Father, I cannot rest at night. I cannot rest in the day. And now I remember that, when I was little, La Mora told me that I would never rest until I found the Three Oranges. I must go and find the Three Oranges."

The King did not want his son to leave him. But the Prince begged so hard that at last the King said,

"Go, my son. Go with God. And return to me when you have found the Three Oranges."

The next day the Prince got on his white horse and off he went. He rode over the mountains. He rode down the valleys. His white horse became lame. So the Prince left his horse with a farmer and went on foot. He walked and he walked. At last he came to an old man who was caring for some black goats. The old man said,

"Where are you going, young man? You have never been this way before."

"I cannot rest," said the Prince, "until I find the Three Oranges."

"You must go on and on," said the old man. "And God go with you."

The Prince went over the mountains and down the valleys. At last he met a man with no hair. The man was leading a black horse. The man said,

"Where are you going, young

man? You have never been this way before."

"I cannot rest until I find the Three Oranges," said the Prince. "Can you tell me where I may find them?"

"I will help you," said the man with no hair on his head. "Take this stone. When you come to the foot of the mountain, throw this stone as far as you can throw it."

The Prince went to the foot of the mountain. He threw the stone as far as he could throw it. And the stone fell into the middle of a river that ran down the valley.

The Prince went to where the

stone fell, and jumped into the water. Down, down he went to the bottom of the river. At the bottom of the river the Prince found a beautiful garden.

In the middle of the garden was a fountain. Beside the fountain was a tree with three oranges growing on one branch.

The Prince knew that the oranges were the Three Oranges that La Mora, the witch, said he must find. As the Prince broke off the branch of the tree with the Three Oranges he fell into the fountain.

The Prince felt as if he were going to sleep. When he opened his eyes, he was sitting on the bank of the river holding a branch with the Three Oranges on it.

The Prince started for his Father's country. He walked over the mountains. He walked down the valleys. It was very hot and dry.

"I must have a drink or I cannot go on," said the Prince to himself. "I will have to eat one of the oranges."

As the Prince cut one of the oranges open, the orange cried,

"Give me water! Give me water! I must have water or I shall die."

But the Prince had no water and the orange died.

The Prince walked on and on. He carried the branch with two oranges upon it. At last he came to an Inn. He got some bread and a bottle of wine and a bottle of water.

The Prince carried the bread and the bottle of wine and the bottle of water with him. He came to a tree and he sat down under it to eat his bread.

"I will cut an orange," said the

Prince to himself. "For now I have water to give the orange."

As the Prince cut the orange open, the orange cried,

"Give me water! Give me water! I must have water or I shall die."

The Prince picked up a bottle to give the orange some water. But he picked up the wrong bottle and poured wine over the orange. The orange died.

The Prince was very sad as he went on his way.

"Two oranges have died and I have only one orange left."

The Prince came to a river that

ran down a valley. He sat on the bank of the river and looked at his one orange.

"Beautiful orange," said the Prince. "I will cut you open and then I shall give you some water."

The Prince cut the orange open and the orange cried,

"Give me water! Give me water! I must have water or I shall die."

The Prince put the orange into the river.

Suddenly out of the river came the most beautiful Princess that the Prince had ever seen. The Prince fell in love with her and wanted her for his wife.

The Prince and the Princess were married and lived very happily in the valley. And in a year they had a beautiful baby son.

"We must go to my father's country," said the Prince. "I want him to see my baby son."

La Mora and the Princess

The Prince and his wife and his baby son went to his father's country. When they came to the gate of the palace the Prince said,

"Wait here by the fountain with our little son. I will go to my father and tell him that I have returned home. And I will tell him of my beautiful wife and my baby son."

"Do not be away from me for long," said the Princess. "I feel that something will happen to me."

"I will help you climb up into

this tree that is by the fountain," said the Prince. "I will not be gone for long and nothing can happen to you, for no one can see you up in the tree."

The Prince helped the Princess up into the tree. And then he gave her the baby to hold.

"I will not be gone for long," said the Prince. And then he went into the palace to see his father, the King.

La Mora, the witch, came to the fountain to get a drink of water. As she leaned over the fountain to get a drink, she saw a beautiful face in the water.

"I have become very beautiful," said La Mora to herself.

La Mora leaned over the fountain to look more closely at the beautiful face. And then she saw her own ugly face beside the beautiful face in the fountain. The witch was very angry. She turned and looked up into the tree.

"Beautiful Princess, come down from the tree. You might let your baby fall into the fountain," said La Mora.

The Princess came down from the tree.

"You have a beautiful child," said La Mora. "And you are a

beautiful mother, for your hair is yellow like the sun. Sit down and let me comb your hair. It is falling about your face."

The Princess sat down by the fountain. La Mora started to comb her hair. But the witch suddenly pushed a pin into the head of the Princess and she was turned into a dove. The dove flew away.

Then La Mora, who was a witch, changed herself to look like the Princess. She took the baby and climbed up into the tree.

Soon the Prince came back with many servants. He helped the

false Princess and the baby from the tree.

"You do not seem the same to me," said the Prince. "What is the matter?"

"I am tired," said the false Princess. "The sun has made my face brown. When I am rested, I will be the same as before."

The Prince took the false Princess and his son to his father. The King was very happy, for he was getting old and he wanted the Prince to be the King. Not long after that, the old King died. The Prince became King of the country. And La Mora, the witch, became Queen.

In the garden of the palace there was an old gardener who looked after the trees and the flowers. Every day, a dove came and sat in a tree. Before long the dove spoke to the gardener.

"Tell me, gardener, what are the King and the Queen doing?"

"The King and Queen eat and drink. They have a happy life."

"Tell me, gardener, what is the baby doing?" said the dove.

"Sometimes the baby cries," said the gardener, "and sometimes the baby sleeps."

"Dear little baby," said the dove. "Its mother cannot look after it. For its mother must fly in the air."

Every day the dove came and spoke to the gardener. And every day the gardener told the dove what the baby Prince was doing. He was growing into a fine little boy.

At last the gardener went to the King and told him that a dove came every day and asked about the Prince.

"Have my servants catch this dove and give it to the Prince for a pet," said the King.

The next day the dove came to the garden and the servants caught it. The servants took the dove to the King.

As soon as the false Queen saw the dove, she wanted to kill it.

But the King said,

"No, you cannot kill the dove. I will take it to my son for a pet."

The dove did not try to fly away and the King told the Prince that he could play with it.

The Prince was happy to have the dove for a pet. He played with the dove all day. He saw that the dove kept scratching its head as if something hurt it. The little boy put his hand on the dove's head. He found a pin sticking into the head. The Prince pulled the pin out of the dove's head.

Suddenly a beautiful lady stood before the Prince.

"Do not be afraid," said the Queen. "I am your own mother. I was changed into a dove by the witch, La Mora."

Just then the King came in to tell his son good night. He saw his own true wife talking to the Prince.

The Queen told the King how

La Mora had pushed a pin into her head and changed her into a dove.

"All these years I have been a dove, sitting in a tree in the palace garden watching over you and my little son," said the Queen. "The gardener has told me all that you did."

The King was very angry and he sent his soldiers to get La Mora. But La Mora, because she was a witch, knew that the soldiers were going to kill her. She turned herself into a raven and flew out of the window.

But La Mora did not know how to change herself back into a woman again. So she had to be a raven for evermore.

The beautiful Queen and the Prince and the King lived happily ever after.

The Three Brothers

Once there were three brothers who lived long, long ago. It was a time when the fairies danced every night in the woods. And the cave men lived in caves in the mountains.

These three brothers lived on a farm near the mountains. One day the youngest brother, whose name was Axular, came home and said,

"I am going away for a year and a day."

"Where are you going?" asked the other two brothers.

Axular did not want to tell his brothers where he wished to go.

"Tell us where you are going and perhaps we will go with you," said the other two brothers.

At last Axular said,

"I am going up into the mountains. There is a cave man who lives in a cave in the mountains. I am going to ask him to teach me the secrets of the fairies."

The two brothers were so surprised that at first they could not say anything. But the oldest brother did not wish the youngest brother to know more than he did. So at last the oldest brother said,

"We will go with you."

The next morning the three brothers started for the mountains. They climbed all day. When the sun was going down, they came to the cave where the cave man lived.

The youngest brother stood before the cave and called,

"We are three brothers. And we have come to ask you to teach us the secrets of the fairies."

The cave man was very angry. He made a noise like thunder. But the three brothers were not afraid. They did not go away.

At last the cave man said, "I will teach you the secrets of the fairies. But you must stay with me for a year and a day. And the last one to leave my cave must be my servant."

"Yes," said Axular. "We will stay with you for a year and a day. And the last one to leave your cave will be your servant."

The oldest brother said to the other, "When the time is up, we will get out of the cave first. We will leave our youngest brother to be the servant of the cave man."

So the other brother said,

"We will stay a year and a day in the cave and learn the secrets of the fairies."

The cave man taught the three brothers all the secrets that he knew. They learned to fly in the air. They learned magic words.

After a year, the cave man said,

"I have taught you all that I know. Tomorrow you must leave."

The three brothers did not sleep that night. Each one was thinking, "I do not want to be the last one to leave this cave. I do not want to be a servant to the cave man."

Axular could hear his two brothers talking together. Axular knew they were planning on leaving him to be the servant of the cave man.

Axular prayed to the Good God, "Father, make the sun to shine brightly tomorrow morning. Make the sun shine brightly through the door of this cave."

The next morning the three brothers heard the cave man calling,

"Get up and be gone from my cave. And the last one to leave my cave shall be my servant."

The three brothers started for the door of the cave through which the sun was brightly shining. Axular was the last one to get to the door.

"You are my servant," cried the

cave man. “You are the last one out of the cave.”

“No! No!” said Axular. “There is one behind me.” Axular pointed to his black shadow which was on the wall of the cave.

The cave man tried to catch the black shadow. And Axular ran out of the cave.

After that, Axular was called The Man Without a Shadow. Even in the sunlight there was no black shadow behind Axular.

The cave man still has Axular’s shadow in the cave in the mountains.

Conchita

Once upon a time a young horse trader went to a village to trade horses. He saw a beautiful girl and fell in love with her. And when he went back to his own village he took this beautiful girl home as his wife.

The young man's mother did not like this beautiful girl from another village. And the sister Juana, who was not beautiful, did not like her brother's wife.

The beautiful wife was good to her husband's mother and to his sister. But they had no kind words for her. In a year the horse trader and his wife had a beautiful baby girl. And the young wife got sick and died.

The young husband was very sad. He left the baby, who was called Conchita, with his mother and sister and went far away to trade his horses. He did not come home often. The little girl grew up with her grandmother and her aunt, Juana. The grandmother died and Conchita was left with her aunt. Conchita was very beautiful, like her mother. But her Aunt Juana did not love her.

Juana made Conchita do all the hard work. Conchita kept the house clean. And she had to go to the spring to get water for Juana. The fountain at the village was nearer than the spring. But Juana said that she liked the cold water from the spring.

The girls of the village would not go near the spring. They said that witches from the mountain were around the spring every night. But no one had ever seen them.

On Conchita's seventeenth birthday, she was very happy. There was to be a dance in the village. She was going with her sweetheart,

Carlos. Perhaps her father would soon be coming home from trading horses. Then she and Carlos were to be married.

Conchita had on her best dress. She was ready to go to the village to meet Carlos and his mother.

"I want a drink of cold water," said Juana. "You must go to the spring and get me a pitcher of water."

"Oh, Aunt Juana," said Conchita, "I am all ready for the dance. If I go to the spring now, I will get hot and tired. My dress and my shoes will be dusty."

"You are a lazy girl just like

your mother. Get the water," said Juana.

Without saying another word Conchita picked up the water pitcher and went to the spring for cold water.

Conchita did not come back from the spring with a pitcher of cold water for her aunt.

At first Juana said to herself, "That bad girl has gone to the dance without getting me a drink of cold water."

Then darkness came and still Conchita had not come back from the spring.

Carlos had been waiting for

hours in the village. He was afraid that Conchita might be sick. At last he went to her house. As soon as Juana opened the door he said,

"Where is Conchita? I have been waiting for her in the village. She did not come to the dance."

Now Juana was very much afraid.

"Hours and hours ago, Conchita went to the spring for a pitcher of cold water. She has not come back," she said.

"Why did you let Conchita go to the spring?" cried Carlos. "You know that the people of the village say that at night the witches come down from the mountain. They dance around the spring."

Carlos ran off to the spring to see if he could find Conchita. And when he got to the spring, he found there the water pitcher filled with water.

It was so dark that Carlos could hardly see. He called and called and called his sweetheart. He could not find Conchita.

"I will have to come again in the morning when the sun is shining," said Carlos to himself. "I cannot see to find Conchita tonight."

The Golden Pitcher

Conchita had hurried to the spring to fill her pitcher with water. After she had filled her pitcher, she suddenly heard horses. She looked up and saw many soldiers riding up the mountain. They looked different from any soldiers she had ever seen.

Conchita was afraid. She knew that the soldiers must be spirits of soldiers who had died long ago when the Moors lived in the castle on the mountain. Conchita hid behind a rock and watched the soldiers ride up the mountain.

When the soldiers had gone, Conchita came out from behind the rock. It was dark now and she could hardly see. She went to the spring to get her pitcher of cold water. There was a light around the spring. And standing in the light was a beautiful woman with long dark hair. The woman looked very sad.

"Can I help you?" asked Conchita.

"Yes," said the woman. "I need your help. Only a good and beautiful girl can help me."

Conchita thought of the dance in the village. She thought of

Carlos, her sweetheart, who would be looking for her. But the woman looked so sad that Conchita was sorry for her.

"I will try to help you," said Conchita.

"For many years I have come to the spring at night," said the woman. "But you are the first young girl that I have ever met at the spring."

"What do you want me to do?" asked Conchita.

"Come with me," said the woman. "Do just as I tell you and you will be safe."

The woman went to a big rock

that was in the side of the mountain. She put her hand upon the rock. The rock moved away and Conchita saw the opening of a cave.

"Shut your eyes and take my hand," said the woman.

Holding the woman's hand, Conchita walked into the cave in the mountain.

Conchita thought that she must be walking a long way inside the mountain. Then the woman said, "Open your eyes."

Conchita found herself standing in a big cave. There was a strange light all around her. The cave shone with the colors of many jewels.

"Sit beside me on this rock and I will tell you my story," said the woman.

"I was a Moor. Long, long ago, I lived in the castle on the mountain. I fell in love with a soldier and we were married. But my father would not forgive me. He put a spell upon me. I could not rest. Even when I died, I could not rest."

"But how can I help you?" asked Conchita.

"The spell my father put upon me will not be broken until I have found a good and beautiful girl who is not afraid. You must hold my hand and pray. As long as you pray, you will be safe. But do not let go of my hand. And do not speak to anyone. At the last, if you will kiss me, the spell will be broken."

"I will try to help you," said Conchita, and she took the woman's hand.

The woman gave Conchita an old pitcher.

"Hold this pitcher in your other

hand. Do not let go of it. It will bring you much happiness."

Conchita was surprised that the hand she held turned into the black paw of a monkey. Conchita remembered what the woman had told her. She held on to the paw and prayed.

Then the cave was filled with monkeys. They pulled at her dress. They pulled at her hair. But Conchita did not stop praying.

The cave grew dark. Conchita could hear horses all around her. She still held onto the black paw and prayed.

Suddenly she heard Carlos calling her.

"Conchita! Conchita! Where are you?"

Conchita was about to call to Carlos and tell him she was inside the cave. But she remembered what the woman had told her. "Do not let go of my hand and do not speak to anyone."

At last the light came back into the cave. The paw that Conchita held grew colder and colder. It was changing its shape. Conchita looked down and saw that she was holding a snake. Conchita shut her eyes and prayed.

Suddenly the snake changed into a stick. The stick was burning. There was flame all about her. In the flames, she saw the face of the woman.

"Kiss me now," said the woman.

Conchita was afraid that the flames would burn her. But she kissed the woman. And then all was darkness.

Conchita was overcome by sleep. When she awoke, she was sitting by the spring. The sun was shining and the birds were singing.

She thought that she had been asleep and having a bad dream. But she looked down and in her hand was a pitcher made of gold.

She heard Carlos calling her as he came running to find her.

"Look, Carlos," said Conchita. "The woman gave me a pitcher of gold. She said that it would bring happiness to us."

Conchita put her hand into the pitcher. It was full of gold money. She told Carlos about the woman in the cave.

"Come away," said Carlos. "I must take you home. I do not want a spell put upon you."

Carlos took up the pitcher of water and Conchita carried the gold pitcher. As they walked home Conchita told Carlos how she had never stopped praying. The monkey and the snake and the flames had not hurt her.

"And now the spirit of the beautiful woman can rest," said Conchita. "At last the spell is broken."

The Silver Spirit

Once upon a time there was a poor man who lived in the mountains. His name was Antonio and he worked for a mule trader.

The mule trader did not pay Antonio very much. Antonio worked hard, but he never had enough money to marry his sweetheart, Rosita.

One day Antonio was taking some mules over the mountains to sell at a village on the other side of the mountains. He was very hot and tired. He sat down to rest and he soon fell asleep.

When Antonio awoke it was night. But a moon shone on the mountains. And down the sides of the mountain there seemed to run a river of silver. The silver shone in the moonlight. On top of the mountain, Antonio saw a man dressed in silver. The man shone in the moonlight with a white light.

Antonio looked at the man for a while but he was so tired that he went to sleep again. But in his sleep he heard someone saying,

"I am the Silver Spirit and I am your friend. Once a year I can show myself to a good and honest man. Remember where you saw the river of silver? Remember, and I will make you rich."

When Antonio opened his eyes, the sun was shining. He looked at the mountain where he had seen the Silver Spirit. But he saw only stones and trees. Antonio looked at the side of the mountain where he had seen the river of silver. He saw only stones and trees. But he saw that his mules were all over the mountainside.

He would have hard work getting them together.

As Antonio drove the mules to the village on the other side of the mountain, he thought of the Silver Spirit.

"If the Silver Spirit can make me rich, I can marry Rosita," said Antonio to himself. "I will try and remember just where I saw the river of silver."

Antonio got to the village and sold his mules. Now he had to go back over the mountains with the money for the mule-trader.

It was almost dark when Antonio

got to the mountain where he had seen the Silver Spirit. He was very tired and he sat down to rest. He remembered what the Silver Spirit had said to him, "Remember where you saw the river. Remember and I will make you rich."

Antonio was going to take the saddle bags off his mule. "You are tired too," he said to the mule. "We will camp here for the night."

Antonio looked up and saw an old man coming toward him.

"Will you help me, for I am very tired?" said the old man.

"Will you lend me your mule, for I have to go up the mountain."

"I cannot lend you the mule, for he belongs to my master, the mule trader. I would have to go with the mule and I am very tired tonight."

"I must see a man who lives upon the mountainside," said the old man. "Let me ride your mule and I will pay you well."

Antonio was very tired but he said to himself, "I should help this old man, for I am younger than he is."

"I will go with you up the

mountainside," said Antonio. "And you can ride upon the mule, but you do not need to pay me."

So the old man got upon the mule and Antonio walked behind. They went up the mountainside.

When they were half way up the mountain, the old man got off the mule.

"I must go on by myself," said the old man. "Camp here for the night. In the morning if I have not come back, go on your way for you will need me no longer."

Antonio looked around him. He saw nothing but rocks. He picked up some of the rocks and he thought of the river of silver. But these rocks did not look like silver. He was going to throw the rock away when he thought he heard someone speaking to him.

"I will pay you well. Remember I am your friend. I will make you rich."

Antonio put the rocks in the saddle bags. He camped with the mule on the side of the mountain.

In the morning the old man had not come back. So Antonio started for his home.

When he got home, Antonio

told his master, the mule trader, about his trip over the mountains. He told him about the dream of the river of silver coming down the mountain. He told him about the Silver Spirit. And he told him about the old man. At last he showed the mule trader the rock he had in the saddle bags.

The mule trader took the rocks to the owner of a silver mine.

"These rocks are very rich in silver," said the owner of the silver mine. "Where did you get them?"

The mule trader went back to

Antonio and asked him where he got the rock. But Antonio would not tell him. Antonio knew that the mule trader was not always an honest man.

"I will tell the owner of the silver mine where I got the rocks," said Antonio, for he knew the owner of the silver mine was an honest man.

Antonio also knew now that the old man had taken him to the right spot to find the rocks. He was so glad that he had helped the old man.

Antonio showed the owner of

the silver mine where he had picked up the rocks. This man was an honest man and he gave Antonio a lot of money.

Antonio and Rosita were married. And Antonio often told her the story of the beautiful Silver Spirit that he had seen upon the mountain.

The Three Princesses

Once upon a time the Moors came from Africa and took the south part of Spain. There was a Moorish king who had a palace at Granada. This King had three beautiful daughters. But the mother of the girls had died.

The wise men had told the King that when his daughters would be old enough to marry, he would have a great deal of trouble with them.

And so the King said to himself, "My daughters shall live in a castle by the sea. No men of the court shall ever see them. Then when they are old enough to marry, I shall pick their husbands and there will be no trouble."

So the three beautiful girls lived in the castle by the sea with their nurse, named Kadiga. Kadiga had at one time been a Spanish lady, a close friend of the girls' mother.

The three Princesses were named Zuleika, Zoraida, and Fatima. They grew up in the beautiful castle. Many maidservants waited upon them. The girls were very happy.

But the Princesses never saw any men but the gardeners who

took care of the flowers and the trees in the castle gardens. And when they looked out of their windows, they saw only the fisher-men going out to sea in their boats.

Year by year, the girls grew more beautiful. Kadiga, the nurse, often told the girls of their beautiful mother who had been a Spanish lady before she had married the Moorish King of Granada.

One day, Zuleika was looking out of the window. She saw a big ship out on the sea.

"Come," called Zuleika to her sisters. "There is a big ship coming in." Zoraida and Fatima came running to the window.

"It is not a fishing boat," said Zoraida.

Zoraida called to Kadiga.

"Come, Kadiga, and tell us about the great boat."

Kadiga came to the window and looked at the big ship.

"It is a ship coming back from a battle," she said. "There are many soldiers upon the ship. And I can see that there are prisoners."

The three Princesses watched the ship. It came to a stop and the men started coming from it in small boats. There were many

Moorish soldiers and they had three prisoners who were in chains. Kadiga said that the three must be Spanish noblemen, they stood so straight and tall.

"I have never seen such a handsome man as the one dressed in red," said Zuleika.

"It is the one dressed in green that I think is most handsome," said Zoraida.

Fatima did not say anything. But she looked at the nobleman dressed in blue, and she thought,

"He is so handsome, and he is a prisoner in chains."

The Trip to Granada

The three Princesses had grown up in the castle by the sea. But one day the Princesses saw from their window three Spanish noblemen who were prisoners of the Moors.

Kadiga, who was old and wise, knew that the girls had fallen in love with the noblemen. She knew that she must tell the King that the girls were old enough to marry.

Kadiga took a basket and into the basket put a beautiful ripe peach, a beautiful ripe pear, and a beautiful ripe apricot. She told a servant to take the basket to the King at Granada.

When the King saw the pear and the peach and the apricot, he knew what Kadiga was trying to tell him. The King said to himself,

"The time has passed so quickly. Now my daughters are old enough to be married. I had better bring them to my court and pick husbands for them."

The King made ready, and he set out for the castle by the sea to get his daughters.

When the King saw his daughters, he knew that they were

the most beautiful women in the world. He said to Kadiga,

"You have taken good care of my daughters as you took good care of their mother. We must take the princesses to the palace at Granada. And no man must see them until I pick their husbands."

All was made ready for the trip to Granada. And the King sent servants ahead with orders for the people.

No man must be upon the road when the King and his party passed. And if any man happened to be on the road, he must fall upon his face.

Zuleika, Zoraida, and Fatima rode with the King in a beautiful carriage. The Princesses enjoyed the trip very much, for they had never seen the country before. But just before they came to Granada, they met a party of soldiers taking the Spanish prisoners to Granada.

The soldiers at once fell with their faces to the ground, for they had heard the orders of the King. But the three prisoners did not fall on their faces. They were the three Spanish noblemen. One was dressed in blue, one was dressed in green, and one was dressed in red.

The three Spanish noblemen looked at the King and his three daughters. And the three Princesses knew that these were the three men that they had seen from their window in the castle.

As the three Spanish noblemen looked upon the three Princesses, they fell in love with them, for they saw that the three Princesses were the most beautiful women in the world.

The King was very angry. He cried,

"Kill those prisoners that did not fall to the ground."

But the three Princesses cried,

"No! No! No! Do not kill these Spanish noblemen."

And Kadiga said to the King,

"Your daughters have never known anything but kindness from you. So do not have these prisoners killed. Put them at hard labor, but do not kill them."

The King changed his order, and the soldiers did not kill the prisoners. The King saw that this made the Princesses very happy.

The King put the Princesses in a tower of the palace. Kadiga and the maidservants looked after them.

The three Princesses were not happy. The King sent them beautiful clothes and beautiful jewels. But they did not want the clothes. They did not want the jewels. Kadiga, the wise old nurse, at first thought that the Princesses might be sick.

Then Zuleika, the oldest said,

"Dear Kadiga, tell us a story about when you were young."

"What did you do at the Spanish court?" asked Zoraida.

"And did you know any Spanish noblemen?" asked Fatima.

Then Kadiga knew that the three beautiful Princesses were in love with the Spanish noblemen who were prisoners.

The Escape

Zuleika, Zoraida, and Fatima, the three beautiful Moorish Princesses, were not happy. They did not eat and they did not sleep. The King, their father, did not know what to do.

The King sent for Kadiga, the wise old nurse, who had looked after the Princesses ever since they were babies. She had been nurse for their mother, who had been a beautiful Spanish lady. But the mother had died when the girls were very young.

"Kadiga," said the King. "Find

out what is the matter with my three daughters. They look sick, and I am afraid that they might die young as their mother did. Do everything that you can to make them well."

Kadiga tried to get the Princesses to talk to her, but they just sat and did not want to talk.

"Let us sing together," said Kadiga.

"We do not want to sing any more," said Zuleika.

"I heard Spanish songs last night," said Kadiga. "It was good to hear songs of my own country."

"Who was singing the Spanish songs?" asked Zoraida.

"The three Spanish noblemen were singing songs of their own country," said Kadiga.

"Oh, tell us about the three Spanish noblemen," cried all three Princesses. "Tell us about them."

"The Spanish noblemen do hard work all day long," said Kadiga. "But at night they sing songs of their own country. It makes me think of the time when I was a young girl in the Spanish court, and your dear mother was my mistress."

The old woman had tears in her eyes as she looked at the three Princesses.

"We want to hear the Spanish songs," said Zuleika.

"Could the Spanish noblemen sing the songs to us?" asked Zoraida.

"Could they come at night and sing under our window?" asked Fatima.

The Princesses were laughing, and they looked so happy that Kadiga said,

"I will see what I can do."

"Take our jewelry and give it to the guard," said Zuleika.

The girls went and got jewels and put them in Kadiga's hands.

Kadiga went to Hussein Baba who guarded the prisoners at night.

"Hussein Baba," said Kadiga, "the three Princesses are shut up in the tower. They are not happy. They have heard that the three Spanish noblemen sing every night. They want to hear their songs."

"The King would cut my head off if I let any man look upon the Princesses," said Hussein Baba.

"The Princesses are in the tower. No man will see them," said Kadiga. "Just let the Spanish noblemen sing their songs under the window."

Kadiga put the jewels into the hands of Hussein Baba.

"The three Princesses send you a present for your kindness," said Kadiga.

So it happened that night that the three Spanish noblemen sang their songs under the window of the palace tower where the three Princesses lived.

Now the three Moorish Princesses were happy again. They dressed in their beautiful clothes. They put on their beautiful jewels. And they sang together once more.

The King was very happy, for his daughters smiled again. He did not know that every night the Spanish noblemen sang under their window. They sang of their love for the three beautiful Princesses in the tower. And from the tower the Princesses sang the song of the rose.

"The Rose is under the leaves and cannot see. But the Rose can hear the song of the birds."

"I will never marry anyone but a Spanish nobleman," said Zuleika.

"I will never marry anyone but a Spanish nobleman," said Zoraida.

Fatima did not say anything, but she smiled to herself. She thought of the Spanish nobleman dressed in blue.

One night, the Spanish noblemen did not come and sing under the window of the tower. The three Princesses cried all night.

In the morning, Kadiga went to Hussein Baba.

"Where are the Spanish noblemen?" asked Kadiga.

"They were prisoners until the King of Spain would pay much money for them. Now the King of Spain has paid the money. They are free, and they are going to their homes in the north of Spain."

Kadiga went into the town. She wanted to get news of the three Spanish noblemen. And she found them in the inn, and told them who she was.

"Will you help us, Kadiga?" cried the three noblemen. "We love the three beautiful Princesses. We wish to marry them and take them to the Spanish court."

"I will take your message to the three Princesses," said Kadiga.

The beautiful Princesses were very happy to get the message from the three Spanish noblemen.

They said they would be very glad to go with them to Spain. So the Princesses got more of their jewels. They gave them to Kadiga and asked her to give them to Hussein Baba for his help in making their escape.

Kadiga went to Hussein Baba. The jewels were so rich that he finally said that he would help the Princesses to escape from the tower. Then Kadiga went and told the three Spanish noblemen to be ready. Hussein Baba was to take the three Princesses through some of the tunnels under the palace. In this way, they would get outside of the walls of the city of Granada.

That night, when all in the palace were asleep, Kadiga put a rope ladder out of the window of the tower. She went down the rope ladder and held it at the bottom.

Zuleika, the oldest of all the Princesses, climbed out of the window and went down the rope ladder. Then Zoraida climbed down the ladder. But when Fatima was to crawl out of the window of the tower on to the top of the rope ladder, she was afraid. She could not make herself do it. The others did their best to get her to come down the ladder, but she was so afraid of doing it that she said she would not go but would have to stay behind. The others could not wait, and Hussein Baba took them to the tunnel.

Kadiga and Zuleika and Zoraida followed Hussein Baba through the tunnels a long way. At last they came out in the woods outside of the city. There the three Spanish noblemen were waiting with horses.

The nobleman in blue was very sad that Fatima could not come, but there was no time to wait.

They all got on the horses and rode away to Spain, leaving Hussein Baba with his pockets full of jewels. Hussein Baba never went back to the palace at Granada.

Fatima would not marry any of the men that her father chose for her. So she lived alone in the tower of the castle until she died.

The Cid

There was a hero of Spain who was called The Cid. Many stories are told of how The Cid fought the Moors in Spain. The Moors had come from Africa to take the castles and the beautiful cities of Spain.

King Alfonso had heard lies that had been told about The Cid. He sent The Cid away from his court. The King said that anyone who gave food or help to The Cid would be killed. The Cid and a few of his men rode through the city and no one spoke to them. They rode out into the country. The Cid wondered how he would get food to feed his men. He spoke to his friend, Antolinez.

"How am I going to feed my men?" said The Cid. "My castle and all my money has been taken by friends of the King who have told him lies about me. How am I going to show King Alfonso that I am loyal to him?"

"Go and fight the Moors," said Antolinez. "Try to drive the Moors out of Spain."

"I would have to have money

to get armor and horses for my men," said The Cid. "And where can I get any money?"

Antolinez and The Cid talked all night while the men slept on the ground around them. When the sun came up, they had made a plan to get money so that The Cid could fight against the Moors.

Antolinez got two big chests. The Cid and his men covered the chests with red leather and used bright nails to hold the red leather to the chests. The chests looked very beautiful, just like the chests in which treasure was kept. Then the men filled the chests with dirt. A big lock was put on each chest.

Antolinez went into the city. He went to a man who had a lot of money to lend.

"The Cid has been sent away from the city," said Antolinez.

"Yes," said the man. "I have heard that the King is angry with The Cid."

"The Cid cannot carry his chests with him," said Antolinez. "They are too heavy. But The Cid needs money so that he can arm his men and go to fight the Moors.

Will you keep his chests and lend him money?"

"Yes," said the man. "I will keep The Cid's chests and lend him money." For the man thought that the chests were full of treasure.

So Antolinez and the money lender went out of the city with bags of money. The money lender gave the money to The Cid and he took the chests covered with red leather back to the city.

Now The Cid had money to feed his men. He had money to buy horses and arms.

When fighting men from other

cities heard that The Cid was going to fight the Moors, they came to him. Before long The Cid was at the head of a small army. The army marched toward the land held by the Moors.

Before long The Cid came to the city of Alcocer. The Cid had only a small army. And there were many Moorish soldiers within the city.

The Cid and his army camped on a hill and watched the city. They camped on the hill for a long time. The soldiers in the city wondered what The Cid was going to do. They had to keep watch day and night.

One morning The Cid and his army went away. But on the hill, they left a big tent.

"Look," cried the soldiers. "The Cid and his army have gone away. They know that the city of Alcocer is too strong for them to take."

The people of the city cried, "Look! Look! There is a big tent upon the hill. There may be many fine things in the tent."

The people and the soldiers opened the gates of the city. They went out to see what was in the big tent. And they left the gates of the city open.

Now The Cid and his army were only hiding. When The Cid saw that the gates of the city were open, he cried,

"Forward! Forward through the gates of the city."

Although The Cid had only a small army, they surprised the soldiers and rode through the gates into the city.

The Cid did not kill the people of Alcocer. He tried to make them his friends so that they would serve him well.

The Cid and his army went from city to city. The Cid took many beautiful horses and much armor. He became very rich. And always he sent some of the beautiful horses to King Alfonso with the message,

"The Cid is always loyal to his King."

And at last, King Alfonso asked The Cid to come back to his court.

How to Say Some Spanish Words

The word divided into syllables	*How to say the word*
Al-co-cer	Al-koh-sehr
Al-fon-so	Al-fon-zoh
An-to-li-nez	An-toh-lee-nez
An-to-ni-o	An-toh-nee-oh
Au-re-a	Oh-ray-ah
Ax-u-lar	Ax-oo-lar
Bel-tram	Bell-tram
Ca-la-min	Kah-lah-meen
Ca-mi-lo	Kah-mee-loh
Car-los	Kar-lohs
the Cid	the Sid
Con-chi-ta	Kohn-shee-tah
Fa-ti-ma	Fah-tee-mah
Hus-sein Ba-ba	Hoos-sain Bah-bah
Juan-a	Hwahn-ah
Jo-se Ma-ri	Ho-say Mah-ree
Ka-di-ga	Kah-dee-gah
La Mo-ra	Lah Moh-rah
Pe-dro	Pay-droh
Zo-rai-da	Zoh-rahee-dah
Zu-lei-ka	Zoo-lay-kah